STORIES FROM THE
FAERIE QUEEN

Eight Fairy Tales for Children

By
Edmund Spenser and Jeanie Lang

Illustrator: Rose Le Quesne

PETRA BOOKS
www.PetraBooks.com

Stories from the Faerie Queen
Eight Fairy Tales for Children

THE FAERIE QUEEN

I should like the crystal ball to shew me what my husband will be like

Stories from the Faerie Queen
Eight Fairy Tales for Children

ABOUT THE FAERIE QUEEN

More than three hundred years ago there lived in England a poet named Edmund Spenser. He was brave and true and gentle, and he loved all that was beautiful and good.

Edmund Spenser wrote many poems, and the most beautiful of all is the one called 'The Faerie Queen.' He loved so dearly all things that are beautiful and all things that are good, that his eyes could see Fairyland more clearly than the eyes of other men ever could.

There are many, many stories in 'The Faerie Queen,' and out of them all I have told you only eight. Some day you will read the others for yourself.

In this little book Miss Rose Le Quesne has made one pretty picture for each story. But when you are old enough to read for yourself 'The Faerie Queen' that Edmund Spenser wrote, you will find that there is a picture on every page.

JEANIE LANG.

Stories from the Faerie Queen
Eight Fairy Tales for Children

CONTENTS

Stories from the Faerie Queen
Eight Fairy Tales for Children

I

UNA AND THE LION

Once upon a time, in a country not far from Fairyland, there lived a king and queen and their daughter, whose name was Una.

Una was one of the most beautiful princesses that ever were seen, and she was as good as she was beautiful.

She and her father and mother loved each other very dearly, and they were very happy together, until a dreadful thing happened in their kingdom and took all their happiness away.

A hideous dragon came from another country, and killed men and women and little children. With its fiery breath it turned the trees and grass and flowers into black ashes, and it slew everybody that it came across.

It would have killed Una's father and mother too, but they and some of their servants shut themselves up in a tower made of brass. The dragon tried very hard to get in and eat them up, but it could not break into a tower so strong.

For seven years the king and queen hid in their tower, while the dragon lay outside.

Many brave knights came and fought with the horrible monster and tried to save the king and queen. But the dragon was stronger than all the knights, and killed every one of them.

At last Una made up her mind to ride to Fairyland and ask the Queen of the Fairies to send one of her knights to kill the dragon.

Una took no soldiers nor servants with her, but a dwarf carried for her the food and clothes she needed, and she rode on a little white ass.

Her dress was of white, but she covered it and her beautiful, shining, golden hair up with a black cloak to show that she felt sad. Her lovely face was very sorrowful, for she was so unhappy at the cruel things the dragon had done, and the danger her dear father and mother were in.

Una safely got to the court of the Faerie Queen, and a young knight, fearless and faithful and true, offered to come back with her to kill the dragon.

His name was George, but on the breast of his silver armour, and on his silver shield, a red cross was painted. So people called him the Red Cross Knight.

The sun shone bright, and the birds sang sweetly, as Una and her knight rode away through the woods that lay between her father's kingdom and the lands of the Faerie Queen.

The knight's great war-horse pranced and champed at its bit, and Una's little donkey put down its dainty feet gently on the grass and wondered at the great big horse and his jingling harness as they went along side by side.

Before they had gone very far a storm came on. The sky grew dark and rain fell heavily, and they would have been drenched had they not found shelter in a thick wood. There were wide paths in this wood, and tall trees whose leafy branches grew so close that no rain could come through.

It was such a beautiful wood, and they were so happy talking together and listening to the birds' sweet song, that they rode along without noticing where they went.

So when the rain stopped and they wished to get back to the open road, they could not find the way. On and on they went, until they came to the mouth of a great dark cave.

The knight sprang from his horse, and giving his spear to the dwarf to hold, went forward to see what might be hidden in the darkness.

'Do not be so rash!' cried Una; 'I know that this is a terribly dangerous place, and that a dreadful monster stays in that black den!'

The frightened dwarf also begged him to come away, but the knight said, 'I should be ashamed to come back. If one is good, one need have no fear of the darkness.'

So into the darkness he went, and in the faint light that came from his shining armour he saw a hideous monster. It had a great ugly head and a long speckled tail like a serpent's, and it rushed at the knight, roaring furiously. He struck at it with his sword, but it wound its horrible tail around him, until he was nearly crushed to death.

Una called to him not to fear, but to strike the monster bravely. And he, smiting it with all his might, cut off its head.

Then Una and he rode joyfully onwards, and, as evening fell, they found a way out of the wood. On the road they met an old man who looked kind and good. He asked them to stay all night in his cottage in a little valley near at hand, and they gladly went.

This old man was a wicked magician, and all he wanted was to do them harm.

When they had lain down to rest, he began to work his magic on them. So well did he do it, that he made the Red Cross Knight believe that Una was very false and wicked, and that the best thing he could do was to go away from her. Very early in the morning the knight made the dwarf saddle his horse, and they went off together and left Una asleep in the house of the wicked magician.

When she awoke and found them gone, Una could only weep bitterly at what seemed to her their cruelty.

She rode after them as quickly as she could, but her little donkey could only go slowly, and in his anger and sorrow the knight had made his horse gallop so fast that she had no chance of overtaking them.

Day after day, up hill and down dale, in woods and on lonely moors, she sought her knight. And her heart was very sad, because he whom she loved had left her so ungently.

One day when she was very tired she lay down to rest under the trees in a thick wood. She took off her black cloak, and her beautiful golden hair fell loosely round her face. Her face was so fair and so full of goodness that it seemed to make sunshine in the shady place.

Suddenly there rushed at her from out of the wood a furious lion. He was hunting for something to kill and eat, and when he saw Una he ran at her greedily, with hungry gaping jaws.

But when it had looked at her lovely face, instead of tearing her in pieces it gently licked her little white hands and feet. And Una's sad heart was so grateful to the noble beast that her tears dropped on him as he did it.

The lion would not leave her. He kept watch while she slept, and when she was awake he followed her like a faithful dog.

He followed her like a faithful dog

Together they wandered on, but never met any one that Una could ask if he had seen the Red Cross Knight.

At last, one evening, they saw a young woman walking up a steep mountain path, and carrying a pot of water on her back. Una called to her, but when the woman looked round and saw a lovely lady and a lion, she got such a fright that she threw down the pot and ran for her life. Her old mother was blind, and they lived in a hut on the mountain, and when she got there she rushed in and shut the door.

Una and the lion followed her, and the lion, with one blow from his strong paw, drove the door in.

The two women were hiding in a dark corner, half-dead from fear. Una tried to comfort them, and asked them if she and her lion might shelter there for the night. When darkness came she lay down, very tired, to sleep, while her lion lay and watched at her feet.

In the middle of the night a knock came to the door. It was a wicked robber, who used to bring the things he stole and give them to those two bad women. The women were so afraid of the lion that they dared not come out of their hiding-place. So the thief, in a rage, burst the door open, and when he did this, the lion rushed at him and tore him in pieces.

Next morning Una rose early and went away with the lion.

When she had gone, the women came out, and when they saw the robber's dead body, they were filled with rage at Una and her lion. They ran after her, calling her bad names, but they could not overtake her.

As they were going home they met the wicked magician. They told him about Una, and he rode quickly after her. By his magic he made himself armour the same as that of the Red Cross Knight, and when Una saw him she thought it was her own true knight come back to her at last. He spoke to her as if he was really her knight, and her heart was filled with gladness.

But she was not the only one who thought that the wicked magician was the Red Cross Knight. Sansloy, a rough and wicked man, whose brother had been killed in a fight with the Knight of the Red Cross, came riding along and met them. When he saw the red cross on the magician's breast he rode at him furiously.

The old magician had to fight, whether he wanted to or not, and Sansloy fought so fiercely that he wounded him and cast him bleeding on the ground. Then Sansloy dragged off his helmet and was going to kill him, when he found, instead of the Red Cross Knight's handsome young face, the wicked old face and grey hair of the magician.

Sansloy was afraid of the magician, so he drew back and did not hurt him more. But when he saw how beautiful Una was, he roughly dragged her off her ass, and made up his mind to take her away with him and make her his wife.

When the lion saw the knight roughly take hold of Una, he made a fierce rush at him, and would have torn him in pieces; but Sansloy beat the lion back with his shield, and when the lion would have torn the shield from him, he drove his sword deep into the lion's faithful heart. With a great roar the noble beast fell dead, and Sansloy threw Una before him on his horse and galloped away with her. She wept and sobbed and begged him to let her go, but Sansloy would not listen. And it seemed as if Una had no friend left, or, at least, no friend that could help her. For the little white donkey trotted after her, afraid of nothing except to be left alone without his mistress.

The darkness fell, and the stars that came out looked down like weeping eyes on Una's sorrow and helplessness.

Sansloy stopped his horse at last and lifted Una down. When she shrank from him in fear, he was so rough that she screamed for help until the woods rang and echoed her screams.

Now in the woods there lived wild people, some of whom were more like beasts than men and women. They were dancing merrily in the starlight when they heard Una's cries, and they stopped their dance and ran to see what was wrong.

When Sansloy saw them, with their rough long hair and hairy legs and arms and strange wild faces, he was so frightened that he jumped on his horse and galloped away.

But the wild people of the woods were more gentle than the cowardly knight. When they saw Una, so beautiful and so frightened and so sad, they smiled at her to show her that they meant to be kind. Then they knelt before her to show her that they would obey her, and gently kissed her feet.

So Una was no longer afraid, and when the wild people saw that she trusted them, they were so glad that they jumped and danced and sang for joy. They broke off green branches and strewed them before her as she walked, and they crowned her with leaves to show that she was their queen. And so they led her home to their chief, and he and the beautiful nymphs of the wood all welcomed her with gladness.

For a long time Una lived with them and was their queen, but at last a brave knight came that way. His father had been a wild man of the woods, but his mother was a gentle lady. He was brave and bold as his father had been. When he was a little boy and lived with the wild people, he used to steal the baby lions from their mothers just for fun, and drive panthers, and antelopes, and wild boars, and tigers and wolves with bits and bridles, as if they were playing at horses. But he was gentle like his mother, although he was so fearless. And when Una told him the story of the Red Cross Knight and the lion, and of all her adventures, his heart was filled with pity. He vowed to help her to escape, and to try to find the Red Cross Knight. So one day he and she ran away, and by night had got far out of reach of the wild men of the woods.

When the wicked magician knew of Una's escape, he dressed himself up like a pilgrim and came to meet her and the brave knight of the forest.

'Have you seen, or have you heard anything about my true knight, who bears a red cross on his breast?' asked Una of the old man.

'Ah yes,' said the magician, 'I have seen him both living and dead. To-day I saw a terrible fight between him and another knight, and the other knight killed him.'

When Una heard this cruel lie she fell down in a faint. The brave young knight lifted her up and gently tried to comfort her.

'Where is this man who has slain the Red Cross Knight, and taken from us all our joy?' he asked of the false pilgrim.

'He is near here now,' said the magician. 'I left him at a fountain, washing his wounds.'

Off hurried the knight, so fast that Una could not keep up with him, and sure enough, at a fountain they found a knight sitting. It was the wicked Sansloy who had killed Una's lion and carried her away.

The brave knight rushed up to him with his drawn sword.

'You have slain the Red Cross Knight,' he said; 'come and fight and be punished for your evil deed.'

'I never slew the Red Cross Knight,' said Sansloy, in a great rage. 'Your enemies have sent you to me to be killed.'

Then, like two wild beasts, they fought, only resting sometimes for a moment that they might rush at each other again with the more strength and fury.

Blood poured from their wounds, the earth was trampled by their feet, and the sound of their fierce blows rang through the air.

Una was so terrified at the dreadful sight that she ran away and left them fighting furiously.

Before she had gone far she saw a little figure running through the woods towards her. It was her own dwarf, and his woful face told her that some evil thing had happened to the Red Cross Knight.

The knight had had many adventures since he left her in the magician's hut, and at last a giant had caught him, and kept him a prisoner in a dreary dungeon. The dwarf had run away, lest the giant should kill him.

Una loved the Red Cross Knight so much that her heart almost broke when she heard the dwarf's story. But she made up her mind to find her knight and free him. So on she went, up hill and down dale, beaten by driving rain and buffeted by bitter winds.

At last, by good chance, she met a knight and his squire. This knight was the good Prince Arthur, of all the knights of the Faerie Queen the bravest and the best. To him she told her sorrowful tale.

'Be of good cheer and take comfort,' said the good prince. 'I will never leave you until I have freed the Red Cross Knight.'

And the prince kept his promise.

The story of St. George and the Dragon will tell you how Una and her knight met together again and were married, and forgot their past sorrows in their great happiness.

II

ST. GEORGE AND THE DRAGON

Long, long ago, before the things that happened were written down in history books, a spiteful fairy came into the castle of an English king. She saw a beautiful baby-boy, the king's little son, lying asleep, and, out of mischief, she ran away with him and left her own ugly little fairy baby there instead.

But when she had stolen the baby, she could not be troubled to take care of him. So she laid him down in the furrow of a ploughed field.

Soon a ploughman, with his horses, came that way. He was a kind man, and he lifted the baby up off the cold brown earth and carried him home to his cottage. He called him Georgos, and brought him up as if he were his own boy.

When Georgos was a big boy he did not care to be a ploughman. He wished to be a knight and fight for people who were not as strong as he was. So he went to the court of the Faerie Queen, and she took him for one of her knights. She called him George, and gave him armour all shining with silver and with a red cross on his shield and on his breast.

You have heard the story of Una, so you know that it was George of the Red Cross who left the fairy court to fight for her and to be her knight.

There was no sadder knight to be found in all Fairyland than George of the Red Cross, after the wicked magician had made him think that Una was false and bad. With a heavy heart he rode away from the magician's cottage in the grey dawn, with the dwarf sadly following him.

As he went through the woods he met a knight riding with a beautiful lady in red robes that sparkled with jewels. The lady's horse was all decked out with gold, and from its bridle hung golden bells.

Although she was so beautiful, she was really a wicked witch, who was never so happy as when she was making men fight and kill each other.

When she saw George coming, she said to the knight with whom she rode, 'Here comes a knight! you must fight with him.'

So the knight rode furiously at George, and George met him as fiercely, and both their spears splintered as they crashed against each other. Then, with their swords they cut and thrust and hacked. The knight cut through a piece of George's helmet by the fury of one blow, but George gave him such a stroke in return, that his sword went through the steel helmet right into the knight's head, and he fell dead.

When the witch saw him fall, she galloped away, screaming with fear. George rode after her and begged her not to be afraid, but the witch pretended to cry bitterly. She told him she did not cry for sorrow that the knight was dead, but only because she was frightened. She said that the knight who lay there had wished to marry her, but that she did not love him, and liked George much better.

The witch looked so beautiful, with her red robes and splendid jewels, and pretended so well to be simple and good, that George believed all that she said.

'Do not be afraid,' he said, 'I will take care of you, and be your friend.'

So he did not think of Una any more, but rode away happily with the witch, who said her name was Fidessa.

In the middle of the day, when the sun had grown very hot, they rested in the shade of two great trees.

The spreading branches of the trees were overgrown with grey moss, and their green leaves were never still, but whispered and trembled as if the wind was blowing on them. George thought he would make a garland of these fresh leaves to put on Fidessa's dark hair. He plucked a little branch, and, as he broke it, red drops of blood trickled down from the place where it was broken.

Then a sad voice spoke out of the tree, and told him that the trees were not really trees, but a knight and a lady, who had been bewitched by the magic of a wicked witch.

The witch who had done it was Fidessa, and when Fidessa heard the tree speak, she was afraid that George would find her out. But George was too simple and too true to think that beautiful Fidessa could be so wicked. He was very sorry for having hurt the tree-man, and with some earth plastered up the place that bled.

Then he and Fidessa hurried away from the place of the shivering trees.

When they had ridden for a long time they came to a gorgeous palace where only bad people stayed. Fidessa made George come with her into the palace, and while they stayed there she got some of the wicked knights of the palace to fight with George and try to kill him. But George was braver and stronger than any of these knights, and instead of their killing him, he killed them.

One day Fidessa went from home, and, while she was away, Una's dwarf, who had never left George, went wandering through the palace.

In a dark and horrible dungeon he found many knights, and kings, and ladies and princes shut up as prisoners.

The dwarf ran and told George, and the Red Cross Knight, fearing that he also would be made a prisoner and cast into the dungeon if he stayed longer in the enchanted palace, rode away. The wounds he had got in his last fight were still unhealed, so that he could not go fast.

When Fidessa got back and found him gone, she rode after him as fast as ever she could.

When she found him he was resting, with his armour off, on the mossy grass by the side of a sparkling fountain. He was peacefully listening to the sweet song of birds, and to the tinkling water, when Fidessa's red robes showed through the trees.

She talked to him so cunningly that soon she persuaded him to think that she loved him very much and meant him nothing but kindness.

Now the witch knew that the water of the fountain was magic water, and if any one drank it all his strength would leave him. So she made George lie down on the sandy gravel and drink. In one minute his strength all went from him and he was no stronger than a tiny boy.

No sooner had this happened than there walked out from amongst the trees an enormous ugly giant. In his hand, for a club, he carried a big oak-tree that he had pulled out of the earth by the roots. When he saw George he rushed at him like an earthquake, and smote him such a mighty blow that George fell fainting to the ground. Then the giant picked him up as if he had been a helpless little baby, and carried him away, and threw him into the darkest dungeon of his castle in the woods.

Una's dwarf, who had hidden in the bushes and seen all that happened, ran away, lest the giant should kill him.

But Fidessa, the wicked witch, made friends with the giant, and he made her his wife.

He gave her a robe of purple and gold to wear, and put a splendid gold crown on her head. And to make people more afraid of her than they were already, he gave her a horrible beast with seven heads and a long scaly tail of brass to ride on.

For months and months George was a prisoner in the gloomy dungeon. The light never came into it, nor any air. He was chained with heavy iron bands, and was given scarcely anything to eat or to drink. His face grew white and thin, and his eyes grew hollow. His strong arms became only skin and bone, and his legs were so feeble that he could not stand. He looked more like a shadow than a man.

One day, as he lay on the floor of the dungeon, feebly moaning and longing to die, the door burst open.

A knight in shining armour of diamonds and gold stood before him, and before George could speak to him, there ran into the dreary cell, like a sunbeam in the dark, his own beautiful Una.

Una nearly cried for joy at seeing her knight again, and for sorrow because he looked so terribly ill.

She told him that Prince Arthur, the knight who had saved him, had cut off the giant's head, and slain the seven-headed monster, and made Fidessa prisoner.

Then Prince Arthur tore off Fidessa's robe of purple and gold, and her golden crown and all her sparkling jewels. And all her beauty faded away, and she looked like the hideous, wicked old witch that she really was.

George shrank away from her in horror, and wondered how she could ever have made him forget Una, or have made him think that she herself was good and beautiful.

And Fidessa, frightened at being found out, ran away and hid herself in a dark cave in the lonely desert.

Then Una took George, who was now no stronger than a little child who has been ill, to an old house not far away from the giant's castle. It was called the House of Holiness.

There lived there a good old lady and her three good and beautiful daughters, and they helped Una to nurse George until he grew strong again.

And as he grew stronger, from the rest and their care and the dainty food they gave him, those ladies of the House of Holiness taught the young knight many things.

He learned to be more gentle than he had been before, and never to be proud nor boastful, and to love nothing that was not wholly good. He learned, too, not to hate any one, nor to be angry or revengeful, and always to be as generous and as merciful as he was brave.

When he was quite strong once more, he went from the House of Holiness to a place where an old hermit stayed, and from him George learned still more of what was good.

George had always thought that he was a fairy's son, but the hermit told him the story of how the bad fairy had stolen him from his father's castle when he was a baby. And although George loved his Faerie Queen and the fairy knights and ladies, he was glad to think that he was the son of an English king.

The old man told him that if, all through his life, he was true, and brave, and merciful and good, one day he should be called a saint. And he would be the saint who belonged especially to all Englishmen and Englishwomen, and to English boys and girls.

'Saint George shalt thou callèd be,
Saint George of Merry England, the sign of victory.'

Then did George, his shining armour with its red crosses, and his sharp sword and glittering spear buckled on again, ride away once more with Una, to kill the dragon and set free the king and queen.

It was a dreary country that they rode through, for the dragon had laid it all waste, but from far away they saw the tower of brass shining in the sun.

As they drew nearer they saw a watchman on the top of the tower gazing across the plain. Day after day for a long, long time he had looked for Una to come back with a knight to slay the dragon. When he saw Una and George crossing the plain, he ran and told the king and queen, and the old king climbed up to the top of the tower to see for himself that the good news was true.

As they drew near the tower, George and Una heard a hideous roaring sound. It filled all the air and shook the ground like an earthquake. It came from the dragon, that was stretched out in the sun on the side of a hill.

When it saw the knight in gleaming armour riding towards it, it roused itself joyfully up to come and kill him, as it had killed all the other knights.

George made Una go to a high piece of ground, from whence she could see the fight, and where she would be out of danger, and then rode to meet the terrible beast.

Half running and half flying, with its great ugly wings, the dragon came swiftly towards him. It was so big that its shadow looked like the dark shadow of a mountain on a valley. Its body was monstrous and horrible and vast, and was all swelled out with rage. It had scales all over it that shone like brass, and that were as strong as steel. Its wings were like big sails, and when it flapped them and clashed its scales, the sound was like the sound of a great army fighting. Its long tail was spotted red and black, and at the end of it two sharp stings stuck out. It had cruel long claws, and its gaping jaws had each three rows of iron teeth, all stained and wet with the blood of the people it had eaten last. It had eyes like flames, and its breath was fire and smoke.

When it rushed at George, George rode hard at it with his spear. But no spear was ever made that was strong enough to pierce that dragon's scales. The spear glanced off from its ugly, speckled breast, but the dragon, furious at the hard thrust that George had given him, lashed out with its tail so furiously that both the horse and his rider were thrown to the ground. Lightly they rose up again, and again George smote with his spear.

Then the dragon, spreading its wings, rose from the ground like a giant bird, and seizing George and his horse in its claws, flew away with them. Right across the plain it flew, then, finding them heavy, it dropped them on the ground. As it did this, George thrust with his spear under the dragon's stretched-out wing, and made a great gaping wound. The spear broke, but the spear-head stuck in the wound, until the dragon, mad with rage and pain, plucked it out with its teeth.

Then did fire and smoke rush out more terribly than before from the jaws of the furious dragon. It lashed its long tail so savagely that it folded in its coils George's foaming horse. The frantic horse, in its struggles to get free, threw George on the ground amongst the horrible blood. But George sprang to his feet, and with his sharp sword struck again and again at the dragon's head. The sword could not pierce it, but the dragon, annoyed at George's fierce attack, thought it would fly out of his reach. But when it tried, the wound George had made in its wing prevented it.

Then its rage at George grew fifty times more furious. It roared till the whole land shook, and it sent out from its inside such blazing flames that George's face was scorched and his armour grew so hot that it burned into his flesh.

George was so tired and so faint and sore, that when he was burned as well, he feared that the end had come. The dragon saw his faintness, and smiting him a tremendous blow with its great tail, it threw him down, and George fell backwards into a pool of water. Now this pool of water was a magic spring. When George fell into it, all his faintness and weariness vanished.

Una, who feared he was dead, saw him spring out of the water even fresher and stronger than he had been at the beginning of the fight.

The dragon could not believe its eyes, and thought that George must be a new knight who had come to fight it.

Before it had got over its surprise, George struck its head so fiercely with his sword, which still dripped from the magic water, that he made a great wound.

The dragon, roaring like a hundred lions, struck at George with the stings on the end of its tail. One of them went right through George's shield, and through his armour, and firmly stuck in his shoulder. Though George was faint with the pain it caused, he hit the dragon's tail such a blow that he hewed off five joints and left only the ugly stump.

Mad with rage, the dragon, belching out smoke and fire, and giving fearful cries, seized George's silver shield in its claws and tried to drag it from him. Again and again, and yet again, George struck at it with his sword. At last he hit the joint and cut the paw clean off. Even then, so tight was the grip that the claws had got, that it still hung bleeding from the shield.

Then was the dragon's rage so frightful, that the flames and smoke from its mouth were like the flames and smoke that pour out of a burning mountain. All the sky was darkened, and as George shrank back in horror from the burning, choking, smelling darkness, his foot slipped in the mire, and he fell.

Now there grew in that land a magic tree, all hung with fruit and rosy apples. From the trunk of the tree there flowed a little stream of sweet balm that could cure even deadly wounds and make weak people strong. The dragon was afraid of this tree and its magic stream, and dared not go near it.

All night George lay as if he were dead, and Una, on the hillside, waited with a heavy heart for morning to come.

He lay so close to the magic tree that the dragon dared not come near him, but it thought that he must have died of his wounds.

When the black night had rolled away and daylight spread over the land, George arose from his sleep. His wounds were all healed by the magic balm, and he was stronger than before.

When the dragon rushed at him with its great fierce mouth gaping wide, George thrust his sword down its throat and wounded it so terribly that it rolled over like a huge mountain in an earthquake. The ground shook as it fell, and the last breaths that it drew stained the beautiful morning sky, like smoke from a furnace.

At first it seemed to Una too good to be true that the dragon was dead. But when the last of the black smoke had cleared away, and the monster lay quite still, she knew that George had won the fight and slain the dragon.

The watchman on the brazen tower had also seen the dragon fall, and so the king had the gates of brass, that had been closed for so long, thrown wide open.

With sounds of trumpets and shouts of joy the king and queen and their people came out to greet George and Una, and to thank George, who had saved them and their land from the horrible dragon.

The people crowded round the dead body of the monster. The children wished to look at it closely, and when a bold little boy took hold of its claws, his mother screamed with fright, and dragged him back. So long had they been in terror of their savage enemy, that even when it lay dead they still feared that it might do them some harm.

The dragon was dead

There never was a happier wedding than the wedding of Una and George, the Red Cross Knight, nor was there ever any bride more beautiful than Una.

Her dress was spotless, like a white lily. It was not made of silver nor silk, yet like silver and silk it shone and glistened. Her golden hair hung round her happy face, and her face was like the freshest flower of May.

Fairy music rang through the air, and there was nothing but happiness in the land on the day that Una wedded brave George of Merry England.

III

BRITOMART AND THE MAGIC MIRROR

Long years ago there lived a beautiful princess whose name was Britomart.

When she was a little girl she did not care to play with dolls nor to sew, but she loved to ride and to play boys' games. And when she grew older she learned to fight with spears and swords like the knights at her father's court.

Now a great magician called Merlin had once given a wonderful gift to the king, Britomart's father.

It was a magic mirror, that looked like a ball of the clearest crystal.

When the king looked in this mirror he saw all that was going to happen to him, and which of his friends were false and which true. There was no hidden secret which that crystal ball could not tell.

One day Britomart went into her father's room and looked into his magic mirror.

'What shall I wish to see?' she asked of herself.

Then she thought, 'Some day I shall marry. I should like the crystal ball to show me what my husband will be like.'

Even as she thought this, she saw, like a moving picture, a knight riding across the crystal.

He was tall and broad and strong, and looked very brave. The front of his shining helmet was drawn up, and from under it looked out the handsome face that his friends loved and his foes feared. He wore beautiful armour, all inlaid with gold, and she knew what his name was, and that he had won this armour in a fight with another great knight, for on it was written:

'Achilles' armes which Artegall did win.'

From that day Britomart could think of nothing but the knight whose picture had ridden across the mirror and vanished away.

She grew thoughtful and sad, and could not sleep, for she feared it was a dreadful thing to love a shadow.

Her old nurse slept in her room, and at night when she heard Britomart tossing about in bed and softly crying to herself, the old woman was very unhappy. Night after night she heard her, till she could bear it no longer. She asked Britomart what was wrong, and Britomart sobbingly told her.

Then the good old nurse comforted Britomart. She said she was sure that Artegall must be a real man, and not just a shadow, and that she would find him. Then she tucked the bedclothes round Britomart, and put out the flickering lamp. When Britomart, much comforted, had fallen quietly asleep, her nurse sat and watched beside her, and dropped some tears because Britomart was no longer a little baby-girl for her to take care of, but a grown-up girl who loved a knight.

Next day the old nurse went to the woods and gathered all sorts of herbs. She boiled them down together, and mixed them with milk and other things, and put them in an earthen pot. Round the pot she bound three of her hairs plaited together. Then she said a charm over the pot, and made Britomart turn round and round and round about it. She thought that this charm would cure Britomart of loving the knight, and make her gay and happy again. But the old nurse's charm was no good. Britomart grew thin and sad and ill.

Then the old woman thought of Merlin, the magician who had made the mirror.

'It is all his fault that my princess is so sad,' she said; 'he must make her happy again.'

So she dressed Britomart and herself in shabby old clothes, and went to seek Merlin.

The magician lived in a dark cave under a rock. The rock lay near a swift-rushing river that ran down between thickly wooded hills. Hollow, fearful sounds, and a clanking, as of chains, were always heard there.

When Britomart and her nurse reached the lonely cave, and heard the noise of moans and groans and clanking chains, they were too frightened at first to go in. But at length they plucked up courage and entered the cave, and found Merlin writing magic words on the dark floor. He knew very well, although they wore shabby old clothes, that his visitors were the Princess Britomart and the princess's nurse. But he pretended that he did not know them, and asked them what they wanted.

'Three moons have come and gone,' said the nurse, 'since this fair maid first turned ill. I do not know what ails her, but if you cannot cure her, she will die.'

Merlin smiled.

'If that is all you want,' he said, 'you had better take her to a doctor.'

'If any doctor could have done her good,' said the nurse, 'I should not have troubled you. But I fear that a witch or a wicked fairy must have bewitched her.'

Then Merlin burst out laughing.

'Why do you go on pretending to me?' he said. 'I know all about it. This is the beautiful Princess Britomart, and you are her nurse.'

At that Britomart blushed rosy red, but the nurse said:

'If you know all our grief, then have pity on us, and give us your help.'

Then Merlin told Britomart not to be sad, for Artegall was a real living knight, and one of the bravest and noblest that lived. His home was in Fairyland, but he was a king's son that the fairies had stolen away when he was a baby.

'You shall marry Artegall,' said the magician, 'and bring him back from Fairyland to his own country, where he shall be king.'

Then he gave her much advice, and told her of the great things that should be done in the days to come by the sons that were to be hers and Artegall's.

And Britomart and her nurse, with happy hearts, came away from the magician's gloomy cave.

'But how shall we seek my knight?' asked Britomart of her nurse. 'How shall we find him?'

The nurse said: 'Let us dress ourselves in some of the armour that your father has taken from his enemies. You shall be a knight, and I will be your squire. Together we will ride to Fairyland and find Artegall.'

When Britomart was dressed in shining armour of silver and gold, she looked a very handsome, tall, young knight. Her nurse dressed her as carefully as she had dressed her long ago in her baby-clothes, and, when all her armour was on, she put into her hand a long spear. It was a magic spear, and there had never yet been born a knight who could sit on his saddle when it struck him.

In the silent night they got on their horses and rode away, no longer a princess and her nurse, but a gallant knight and a little old squire, who seemed to find his big shield much too heavy for him.

Before Britomart and her nurse had ridden very far, they saw two knights riding towards them. These were Guyon and the Red Cross Knight.

Guyon rode furiously at Britomart, but Britomart rode as furiously at him with her magic spear. And, for the first time in his life, Guyon found himself thrown from his horse and sitting heavily down on the ground. He was very much ashamed and very angry, and would have rushed at Britomart with his sword. But the old palmer, who was with him, calmed his rage, and he made friends with Britomart. And for some time Britomart and those two brave knights rode on together, and shared fights and adventures.

One day as they rode together, Britomart asked the Red Cross Knight if he knew a wicked knight called Artegall.

'He is not a wicked knight,' said the Red Cross Knight angrily. 'He is one of the bravest and the best.'

Britomart was so glad to hear him say this of Artegall, that she could scarcely hide her joy. But she went on pretending that she thought Artegall bad and cruel, just that she might hear his friend praise him.

'There is no knight more brave than Artegall,' said the Red Cross Knight. 'Ladies who suffer wrong, and little children who have none to care for them, are always sure of having Artegall to fight for them. He is as good as he is brave, and as brave as he is good.'

Britomart loved the Red Cross Knight because he was so true to his friend, and more than ever she loved Artegall, the knight of the Mirror.

Presently her way and that of the Red Cross Knight parted, and she rode on with her squire until they came to the sea-shore.

The sea was beating against the rocks, and moaning as it cast itself against the high crags.

Britomart made her old nurse unlace her helmet, and sat down and watched the cold grey waves.

'I feel like a little boat beaten about by the sea,' she said. 'When shall I ever reach my harbour, and find the knight I seek?'

For a long time she sat, sadly thinking. But at last she saw a knight cantering along the sand, and quickly put on her helmet and leaped on her horse, and rode to meet him.

He was a bold knight, and told her to fly, or he would kill her.

'*Fly!*' proudly said Britomart. 'Words only frighten babies. I will not fly. I will fight you!'

Then they fought, and with her spear Britomart gave the knight a terrible wound, and rode away, leaving him lying senseless on the shore.

Many other fights had Britomart as she sought Artegall, and always her magic spear made her the winner.

One day she came to a place where a great many knights were having a tournament.

A beautiful golden girdle, sparkling with jewels, was to be the prize for the knight that fought the best.

For three days they had fought and fought, until the ground was strewed with broken spears and swords.

On the last day of the tournament a stranger knight had appeared. His armour did not shine with silver and gold like those of the other knights, but looked like an old tree all overgrown with moss. His horse was decked with oak-leaves, and he carried a battered old shield.

'The Savage Knight,' the others called him, and they would have laughed at him and his shabby armour, had he not fought so well. All day long he fought, and one knight after another he threw wounded or dead on the ground. At sunset they feared him as they might have feared a fierce lion, and none dared stand against him.

Just then Britomart rode up with her golden armour gleaming against the sunset sky.

She couched her spear and rode at the Savage Knight, and threw him to the ground.

The other knights then all rode at her, but them, too, she threw down with her magic spear.

So they had to own that Britomart was the victor, and had won the golden girdle.

Now the Savage Knight was not really a savage knight. He was no other than Artegall, the knight of the Crystal Ball.

Artegall was so ashamed, and so angry with Britomart for having thrown him from his horse, that when the tournament was over, he rode away to a wood, through which he knew that Britomart must pass.

'The stranger knight with his magic spear shall fight me once again,' he angrily said, 'and this time he shall not be the victor.'

Presently, as he sat under the trees, and watched his horse grazing, he saw Britomart riding up, brave and fearless, in her golden armour.

Artegall sprang on his horse, and furiously rode at Britomart with his steel-headed lance. But, in the twinkling of an eye, he found himself lying on the turf, again unseated by the magic spear.

He rushed at Britomart then with his sword, and cut and thrust at her so savagely that her horse backed away from him. At last he struck a great blow at her head, and the sword, glancing down her armour, struck her horse with such force on its back that it fell to the ground, and Britomart had to jump off. She threw aside her spear and furiously smote Artegall with her sword. She cut his armour through, and wounded him so deeply that blood from his wound streamed to the ground. The blows from Artegall's sword fell on her like hail, but she struck him as fiercely as he struck her. The grass got trampled down and stained with blood, yet still they smote and thrust and smote again.

At last Artegall grew very tired, and Britomart was more tired still. When Artegall saw how tired she was, he gathered up all his strength and struck her a terrific blow, hoping to kill her quite. But the blow only sheared off the front part of her helmet, and left her face uncovered.

And as Artegall's arm rose again for another deadly stroke, it stopped short in the air. For instead of the grim face of the fierce knight he thought he was fighting, there looked out a face that Artegall thought was the loveliest he had ever seen.

Britomart's cheeks were hot and pink, and her hair, that was so long that it reached her feet, had burst from its band and framed her fair face like a golden frame.

The sword slipped from Artegall's fingers to the ground. He knelt at Britomart's feet and begged her to forgive him for having treated her so roughly.

But Britomart was still angry with him for that last fierce stroke of his.

'Rise!' she said, 'or I shall kill you!' and she held her sword over his head.

But Artegall would not rise, but only prayed her the more earnestly to forgive him.

Then the old nurse drew near and begged Britomart to have a truce.

'Rest yourself for a little,' she said, 'and let the Savage Knight rest too.'

Britomart agreed, and the knight raised the front of his helmet that he might breathe more freely.

When Britomart saw his face, so handsome and so brave, she knew at once that the Savage Knight that she had tried to kill was Artegall, the knight of the Mirror.

Her arm dropped, and her sword fell from her hand.

She tried to speak roughly to him, but her tongue would not say the words.

Together they rode off to a castle, where they stayed till they were rested and their wounds were healed.

And each day that they were together Artegall loved Britomart more and more, until at last he could stay no longer silent, but told her that he loved her more than all the world.

So it was that the beautiful princess Britomart found her husband, the gallant knight of the Magic Mirror.

IV

THE QUEST OF SIR GUYON

Long ago, on the first day of every year, the Queen of the Fairies used to give a great feast.

On that day all the bravest of her knights came to her court, and when people wanted help to slay a dragon or a savage beast, or to drive away a witch or wicked fairy, they also came and told their stories.

To one of those feasts there came an old palmer dressed in black. His hair was grey, and he leaned heavily on his long staff. He told a sad tale of the evil things done in his land by a wicked witch.

The Faery Queen turned to Guyon, one of the bravest and handsomest of her young knights. 'You shall go with this old man and save his land,' she said to him.

'I am not worthy,' said Sir Guyon, 'but I will do your bidding and my best.'

So he rode away with the palmer. His good horse had never paced so slowly before, for Guyon made him keep step with the feeble old man.

It was not possible to go far from the fairy court without having fights and adventures, but in every fight Guyon was the victor, because he listened to what the good old palmer said, and did not think that he himself knew better.

One day they came to a wide river on which floated a little boat, all decked out with green branches. In it sat a fair lady, who sang and laughed and seemed very happy and very gay. She was a servant of the wicked witch for whom Guyon was looking, but this Guyon did not know. She offered to ferry Guyon across the river, but she said there was no room in her boat for the palmer.

Guyon thought she looked so pretty and merry, and so kind, that he gladly went with her.

Together they gaily sailed down the river. When the birds sang, she sang along with them, and when little waves gurgled and laughed against the side of the boat, she laughed too.

But soon Guyon found that she was not really good, and he loved her gay laugh no longer, and presently left her and wandered on alone in the island to which she had brought him.

At last he came to a gloomy glen where trees and shrubs grew so thickly that no sunlight could get in. Sitting there in the darkness he found a rough and ugly man. His face was tanned with smoke and his eyes were bleared. Great heaps of gold lay about him on every side. When he saw Guyon, he dashed in a great fright at his money, and began to try to pour it into a hole and hide it, lest Guyon should steal it from him.

But Guyon ran quickly at him and caught him by the arm.

'Who are you,' he asked, 'who hide your money in this lonely place, instead of using it rightly or giving it away?'

To which the man answered, 'I am Mammon, the Money God. I am the greatest god beneath the sky. If you will be my servant, all this money shall be yours. Or if this be not gold enough for you, a mountain of gold, ten times more than what you see, shall be your very own.'

But Guyon shook his head. 'I want none of your gold,' said he.

'Fair shields, gay steeds, bright arms be my delight, Those be the riches fit for an adventurous knight.'

Then said the Money God, 'Money will buy you all those things. It can buy you crowns and kingdoms.'

'Money brings wars and wrongs, bloodshed and bitterness,' said Guyon. 'You may keep your gold.'

The Money God grew angry then.

'You do not know what you refuse,' he said. 'Come with me and see.'

Guyon the fearless followed him into the thickest of the bushes and down a dark opening in the ground.

On and on they went through the darkness. Ugly things came and glared at them, and owls and night ravens flapped their wings, but Guyon had no fear.

At length they came to a huge cave whose roof and floor and walls were all of gold, but the gold was dimmed by dust and cobwebs. A light like the light of the moon from behind a dark cloud showed Guyon great iron chests and coffers full of money, but the ground was strewn with the skulls and dry bones of men who had tried to get the gold, and who had failed and perished there.

Great heaps of gold lay about him on every side

'Will you serve me now?' asked Mammon. 'Only be my servant, and all these riches shall be yours.'

'I will not serve you,' answered Guyon. 'I place a higher happiness before my eyes.'

Then Mammon led him into another room where were a hundred blazing furnaces.

Hideous slaves of the Money God blew bellows and stirred the flames, and ladled out of huge caldrons on the fires great spoonfuls of molten gold. When they saw Guyon in his shining armour, they stopped their work and stared at him in fear and amazement. Never before had they seen any one who was not as horrible and as ugly as themselves. Once again Mammon offered him the gold he saw, but again Guyon refused it.

Then did he bring him to a place where was a gate of beaten gold. Through this gate they passed, and Guyon found himself in a vast golden room, upheld by golden pillars that shone and sparkled with precious stones.

On a throne in this room sat a beautiful lady, dressed in clothes more gorgeous than any that the greatest king on earth ever wore.

'That is my daughter,' said Mammon. 'She shall be your wife, and all these treasures that are too great to be counted shall be yours, if only you will be my servant.'

'I thank you, Mammon,' said Guyon, 'but my love is given to another lady.'

The Money God was full of rage, yet still he thought that he might win Guyon to his will. He took him to a garden where dark cypresses hung their heads over the flaming blossoms of poppies that made men sleep for ever, and where every sort of poisonous flower and shrub flourished richly. It was called the Garden of Proserpine.

The most beautiful thing in the garden was a great tree, thickly leaved and heavily hung with shining golden apples. The branches of the tree hung their golden fruit over a dark river.

When Guyon went to the river's brink and looked in, he saw many men struggling and moaning in the dark and fearful water. Some were trying to grasp the fruit that hung just beyond their reach, and others were trying vainly to get out.

'You fool!' said Mammon, 'why do you not pick some of the golden fruit that hangs so easily within your reach?'

But Guyon, although for three long days and nights he had been without sleep and meat and drink in the dark land of the Money God, was too true and good a knight to do what Mammon wished. Had he picked the fruit, he would have put himself in Mammon's power, and at once been torn into a thousand pieces.

'I will not take the fruit,' he said; 'I will not be your slave.'

And then, for days and days, Guyon knew no more.

When he came to himself and opened his eyes, he found that his head was resting on the knee of the good old palmer.

After the witch's beautiful servant had rowed Guyon away, the palmer had tried and tried to find a means of crossing the river, until at last he succeeded.

Day after day he sought Guyon, until one day a fairy voice called to him, loud and clear, 'Come hither! hither! oh come hastily!'

He hurried to the place from whence the voice came, and in the dark thicket where Mammon had sat and counted his gold, he found Guyon lying.

A beautiful spirit with golden hair and shining wings of many colours, like the wings of a lovely bird, sat by

Guyon's side, keeping all enemies and evil things far from him.

When Guyon felt able for the journey, he and the palmer went on with their travels, and he had many fights and many adventures. But ever after he had been tempted to be Mammon's slave and had resisted him, he was a better and a braver knight.

All his battles ended in victories, and he helped all those who needed help, and at last he and the palmer reached the shore of the sea across which was the land of the wicked witch.

They got a little boat, and a boatman to row them, and for two days they were far out at sea.

On the morning of the third day, Guyon and the others heard the sound of raging water. In the trembling light of the dawn that was spreading across the sea they saw great waves casting themselves high into the sky.

It was a gulf, called the Gulf of Greediness, and in its furious waves many ships were wrecked. But the palmer steered so straight and well that he guided the little boat without harm through the angry seas.

On one side of the gulf was a great black rock where screaming seamews and cormorants sat and waited for ships to be wrecked. It was a magic rock, and the water round it tried to draw Guyon's boat against its ragged sides, that it might be smashed to pieces like the other boats and ships whose broken fragments tossed up and down in the tide.

But so wisely did the palmer steer, and so strongly did the boatman row, that they safely passed the magic rock and got into calm water. And still the boatman rowed so hard that the little boat cut through the water like a silver blade, and the spray dashed off the oars into Guyon's face.

'I see land!' at last called Guyon.

On every side they saw little islands. When they got nearer they found that they looked fresh and green and pleasant. Tall trees with blossoms of white and red grew on them.

'Let us land!' cried Guyon.

But the boatman shook his head.

'Those are the Wandering Islands,' he said. 'They are magic islands, and if any one lands on one of them he must wander for ever and ever.'

On one island sat a beautiful lady, with her long hair flowing round her. She beckoned and called to them to come on shore, and when they would not listen she jumped into a little boat and rowed swiftly after them.

Then Guyon saw that it was the wicked witch's beautiful servant, and they took no notice of her. So she got tired of coaxing, and went away, calling them names.

A terrible whirlpool, where the waves rushed furiously round and round, was the next danger that they met. Then, when they were free of that, a great storm arose, and every fierce and ugly fish and monster that ever lived in the sea came rushing at the boat from out the foaming waves, roaring as if they were going to devour them.

'Have no fear,' said the palmer to Guyon. 'These ugly shapes were only made by the wicked witch to frighten you.'

With his palmer's staff he smote the sea. The waves sank down to rest, and all the ugly monsters vanished away.

When the storm had ceased they saw on an island a lady, who wept and wailed and cried for help.

Guyon, who was always ready to help those who wanted help, wished at once to go to her.

But the palmer would not let him.

'She is another of the servants of the witch,' he said, 'and is only pretending to be sad.'

They came then to a peaceful bay that lay in the shadow of a great grey hill, and from it came the sweetest music that Guyon had ever heard.

Five beautiful mermaids were swimming in the clear green water, and the melody of their song made Guyon long to stop and listen. They had made this song about Guyon:

'O thou fair son of gentle fairy,
Thou art in mighty arms most magnified
Above all knights that ever battle tried.
O! turn thy rudder hitherward awhile,
Here may thy storm-beat vessel safely ride.
This is the port of rest from troublous toil,
The world's sweet inn from pain and wearisome turmoil.'

The rolling sea gently echoed their music, and the breaking waves kept time with their voices. The very wind seemed to blend with the melody and make it so beautiful that Guyon longed and longed to go with them to their peaceful bay under the grey hill. But the palmer would not let him stop, and the boatman rowed onwards.

Then a thick, choking, grey mist crept over the sea and blotted out everything, and they could not tell where to steer. And round the boat flew great flocks of fierce birds and bats, smiting the voyagers in their faces with wicked wings.

Still the boatman rowed steadily on, and steadily the palmer steered, till the weather began to clear. And, when the fog was gone, they saw at last the fair land to which the Faerie Queen had sent Guyon, that he might save it from the magic of the wicked witch.

When they reached the shore the boatman stayed with his boat, and Guyon and the palmer landed. And the palmer was glad, for he felt that their task was nearly done.

Savage, roaring beasts rushed at them as soon as they reached the shore. But the palmer waved his staff at them, and they shrank trembling away. Soon Guyon and his guide came to the palace of the witch.

The palace was made of ivory as white as the foam of the sea, and it glittered with gold. At the ivory gate stood a young man decked with flowers, and holding a staff in his hand. He impudently held out a great bowl of wine for Guyon to drink. But Guyon threw the bowl on the ground, and broke the staff with which the man worked wicked magic.

Then Guyon and the palmer passed on, through rich gardens full of beautiful flowers, and came to another gate made of green boughs and branches. Over it spread a vine, from which hung great bunches of grapes, red, and green, and purple and gold.

A beautiful lady stood by the gate. She reached up to a bunch of purple grapes, and squeezed their juice into a golden cup and offered it to Guyon. But Guyon dashed the cup to the ground, and left her raging at him.

Past trees and flowers and clear fountains they went, and all the time through this lovely place there rang magic music. Sweet voices, the song of birds, the whispering winds, the sound of silvery instruments, and the murmur of water all blended together to make melody.

The farther they went, the more beautiful were the sights they saw, and the sweeter the music.

At last, lying on a bed of red roses, they found the wicked witch.

Softly they crept through the flowery shrubs to where she lay, and before she knew that they were near, Guyon threw over her a net that the palmer had made. She struggled wildly to free herself, but before she could escape, Guyon bound her fast with chains.

Then he broke down and destroyed the palace, and all the things that had seemed so beautiful, but that were only a part of her wicked magic.

As Guyon and the palmer led the witch by her chains to their boat that waited by the shore, the fierce beasts that had attacked them when they landed came roaring at them again.

But the palmer touched each one with his staff, and at once they were turned into men. For it was only the witch's magic that had made them beasts. One of them, named Gryll, who had been a pig, was angry with the palmer, and said he had far rather stay a pig than be a man.

'Let Gryll be Gryll, and have his hoggish mind,
But let us hence depart whilst weather serves and wind,'

said the palmer.

So they sailed away to the fairy court, and gave their wicked prisoner to the queen to be punished.

And Sir Guyon was ready once again to do the Faerie Queen's commands, to war against all evil things, and to fight bravely for the right.

V

PASTORELLA

Long, long ago, in a far-away land, there lived a great noble, called the Lord of Many Islands. He had a beautiful daughter named Claribel, and he wished her to marry a rich prince.

But Claribel loved a brave young knight, and she married him without her father's knowledge.

The Lord of Many Islands was fearfully angry when he found out that she was married.

He threw the young knight into one dark dungeon and Claribel into another, and there they were imprisoned for years and years, until the Lord of Many Islands was dead. Claribel was rich then, and she and her husband would have been very happy together, but for a great loss that they had had.

While she was in prison a little baby girl came to Claribel. She feared that her angry father might kill the baby if he knew that it had been born, so she gave it to her maid, and told her to give it to some one to take care of.

The maid carried the child far away to where there were no houses, but only wild moors and thick woods. There was no one there to give it to, but she dared not take it back in case its grandfather might kill it. She did not know what to do, and she cried and cried until the baby's clothes were quite wet with her tears.

It was a very pretty baby, and the maid noticed that on its little breast there was a tiny purple mark, as if some one had painted on it an open rose. She drew its clothes over the mark, and then laid the baby gently down behind some green bushes, and went home crying bitterly.

When the baby found herself lying out in the cold with no one to care for her, she cried too. And she cried so loudly and so long, that a shepherd called Melibœus heard her cries, and came to see what was wrong.

When he found the beautiful baby, he wrapped her in his warm cloak and carried her home to his wife. From that day the baby was their little girl. They called her Pastorella, and loved her as if she were really their own.

Pastorella grew up amongst shepherds and shepherdesses, yet she was never quite like them. None of the shepherdesses were as beautiful as she was, and none were as gentle nor as full of grace. So they called Pastorella their queen, and would often crown her with garlands of flowers.

When Pastorella was grown up, there came one day to the country of plains and woods where she lived a brave and noble knight.

His name was Calidore, and of all the knights of the Faerie Queen there was none so gentle nor so courteous as he. He always thought of others first, and never did anything that he thought would hurt the feelings of any one. Yet he was brave and strong, and had done many gallant deeds.

He was hunting a monster that had done much harm, when he came near the home of Pastorella.

Sheep were grazing on the plain, and nibbling the golden buds that the spring sunshine had brought to the broom. Shepherds were watching the sheep. Some were singing out of the happiness of their hearts, because of the blue sky and the green grass and the spring flowers. Others were playing on pipes they had made for themselves out of the fresh young willow saplings.

Calidore asked them if they had seen the monster that he sought.

'We have seen no monster, nor any dreadful thing that could do our sheep or us harm,' they answered, 'and if there be such things, we pray they may be kept far from us.'

Then one of them, seeing how hot and tired Sir Calidore was, asked him if he would have something to drink and something to eat. Their food was very simple, but Calidore thanked them, and gladly sat down to eat and drink along with them.

A little way from where they sat, some shepherds and shepherdesses were dancing. Hand in hand, the pretty shepherdesses danced round in a ring. Beyond them sat a circle of shepherds, who sang and piped for the girls to dance. And on a green hillock in the middle of the ring of girls sat Pastorella. She wore a dainty gown that she herself had made, and on her head was a crown of spring flowers that the shepherdesses had bound together with gay silken ribbons.

'Pastorella,' sang the shepherds and the girls, 'Pastorella is our queen.'

Calidore sat and watched. And the more he looked at Pastorella, the more he wanted to look. And he looked, and he looked, and he looked again at Pastorella's sweet and lovely face, until Pastorella had stolen all his heart away.

He forgot all about the monster he was hunting, and could only say to himself, as the shepherds had sung, 'Pastorella ... Pastorella ... Pastorella is my queen.'

All day long he sat, until the evening dew began to fall, and the sunset slowly died away, and the shepherds called the sheep together and drove them home.

As long as Pastorella was there, Calidore felt that he could not move. But presently an old man with silver hair and beard, and a shepherd's crook in his hand, came and called to Pastorella, 'Come, my daughter, it is time to go home.'

It was Melibœus, and when Calidore saw Pastorella rise and call her sheep and turn to go, he did not know what to do, for he could only think of Pastorella.

But when good old Melibœus saw the knight being left all alone, and the shadows falling, and the trees looking grey and cold, he said to him, 'I have only a little cottage, turfed outside to keep out the wind and wet, but it is better to be there than to roam all night in the lonely woods, and I bid you welcome, Sir Knight.'

In the middle of the ring of girls sat Pastorella

And Calidore gladly went with him, for that was just what he was longing to do.

All evening, as he listened to the talk of Melibœus, who was a wise and good old man, Calidore's eyes followed Pastorella. He offered Melibœus some gold to pay for his lodging, but Melibœus said, 'I do not want your gold, but, if you will, stay with us and be our guest.'

So, day after day, Calidore stayed with the shepherds. And, day after day, he loved Pastorella more. He treated her and said pretty things to her as knights were used to treat and to speak to the court ladies. But Pastorella was used to simpler things, and liked the simple things best.

When Calidore saw this, he laid aside his armour and dressed himself like a shepherd, with a crook instead of a spear. Every day he helped Pastorella to drive her sheep to the field, and took care of them and drove away the hungry wolves, so that she might do as she liked and never have any care, knowing that he was there.

Now, one of the shepherds, whose name was Corydon, for a long time had loved Pastorella. He would steal the little fluffy sparrows from their nests, and catch the young squirrels, and bring them to her as gifts. He helped her with her sheep, and tried in every way he knew to show her that he loved her.

When he saw Calidore doing things for Pastorella he grew very jealous and angry. He sulked and scowled and was very cross with Pastorella.

One day when the shepherd who piped the best was playing, the other shepherds said that Calidore and Pastorella must dance. But Calidore put Corydon in his place, and when Pastorella took her own garland of flowers and placed it on Calidore's head, Calidore gently took it off and put it on Corydon's.

Another time, when the shepherds were wrestling, Corydon challenged Calidore to wrestle with him. Corydon was a very good wrestler, and he hoped to throw Calidore down. But in one minute Calidore had thrown Corydon flat on the ground. Then Pastorella gave the victor's crown of oak-leaves to Calidore. But Calidore said 'Corydon has won the oak-leaves well,' and placed the crown on Corydon's head.

All the shepherds except Corydon soon came to like Calidore, for he was always gentle and kind. But Corydon hated him, because he thought that Pastorella cared for Calidore more than she cared for him.

One day Pastorella and Corydon and Calidore went together to the woods to gather wild strawberries. Pastorella's little fingers were busy picking the ripe red fruit from amongst its fresh green leaves, when there glided from out the bushes a great beast of black and yellow, that walked quietly as a cat and had yellow, cruel eyes.

It was a tiger, and when Pastorella heard a twig break under its great pads, and looked up, it rushed at her fiercely. Pastorella screamed for help, and Corydon, who was near her, ran to see what was wrong. But when he saw the savage tiger, he ran away again in a fearful fright. Calidore was further off, but he, too, ran, and came just in time to see the tiger spring at Pastorella. He had no sword nor spear, but with his shepherd's crook he struck the tiger such a terrific blow, that it dropped, stunned, to the ground. Before it could rise, he drew his knife and cut off its head, which he laid at Pastorella's feet.

From that day Pastorella loved Calidore, and he and she were very, very happy together.

It chanced that one day Calidore went far into the forest to hunt the deer. While he was away a band of wicked robbers attacked the shepherds. They killed many of them, and took the rest prisoners. They burned down all their cottages, and stole their flocks of sheep.

Amongst those that they drove away as captives were Melibœus and his wife, Corydon, and Pastorella. Through the dark night they drove them on, until they came to the sea. On an island near the coast was the robbers' home. The island was covered with trees and thick brushwood, and the robbers lived in underground caves, so well hidden amongst the bushes that it was hard to find them. The robbers meant to sell the shepherds and shepherdesses as slaves, but until merchants came to buy them they kept their prisoners in the darkest of the caves, and used them very cruelly.

One morning the robber captain came to look at his captives. When he saw Pastorella in her pretty gown, all soiled now and worn, with her long golden hair and beautiful blue eyes, and her face white and thin with suffering, he thought her so lovely that he determined to have her for his wife.

From that day she was kindly treated. But when the robber told Pastorella that he loved her and wanted her for his wife, she pretended she was ill.

'I am much too ill to marry any one,' she said.

To the island there came one day the ships of some merchants who wished to buy slaves. They bought Melibœus and Corydon and all the others. Then one of the robbers said to the captain:

'They are all here but the fair shepherdess.'

And he told the merchants that Pastorella would make a much more beautiful slave than any of those they had bought.

Then the captain was very angry.

'She belongs to me,' he said. 'I will not sell her.'

To show the merchants that Pastorella was ill and not fit to be a slave, at last he sent for her.

The cave was lighted only by flickering candles, and Pastorella's fair face looked like a beautiful star in the darkness. Although she was so pale, she was so beautiful that the merchants said that they must certainly have her.

'I have told you I will not sell her,' said the captain sulkily.

They offered him much gold, but still he would only say, 'I will not sell her.'

'If you will not sell this slave,' said the merchants, 'we will not buy any of the others.'

Then the other robbers grew very angry with their captain, and tried to compel him to give in.

'I shall kill the first who dares lay a hand on her!' furiously said the captain, drawing his sword.

Then began a fearful fight. The candles were knocked down, and the robbers fought in the dark, no man knowing with whom he fought.

But before the candles went out, the robbers in their fury killed all their prisoners, lest they might take the chance of escaping, or fight against them. Old Melibœus and his wife were slain, and all the other shepherds and shepherdesses, excepting Corydon and Pastorella.

Corydon, who was always good at running away, escaped in the darkness.

The robber captain put Pastorella behind him, and fought for her. At last he was stabbed through the heart and fell dead. The sword that killed him pierced Pastorella's arm, and she, too, fell down in a faint.

When she opened her eyes the robbers who were left had stopped fighting, and had lighted the candles, and were counting their dead and wounded. When she saw her dear father and mother and her friends lying cold and still beside her, she began to sob and cry. As soon as the robbers knew that she lived, they thrust her back into the darkest of their caves. The most cruel of all the robbers was her gaoler. He would not allow her to bind up her wound, and he gave her scarcely anything to eat or to drink. He would not even let her rest, and so, in pain and hunger and sadness, Pastorella passed her weary nights and days.

Now when Calidore got back from his hunting, he expected to hear the shepherds' pipes, and their songs, and the bleating of the sheep, and to see Pastorella in her dainty gown and with flowers in her golden hair coming to meet him.

Instead of that, the place which had been so gay was sad and silent. The cottages were smouldering black ruins, and there was no living creature there.

Calidore wildly sought everywhere for some trace of Pastorella. But when he sought her in the woods and called 'Pastorella ... Pastorella ...', only the trees echoed 'Pastorella.' In the plains he sought her, but they lay silent and lonely under the stars, and they, too, only echoed 'Pastorella ... Pastorella....'

Week after week he searched for her, until one day he saw a man running across the plain. The man's hair was standing up on his head as if he were in a terrible fright, and his clothes were in rags.

When he got near, Calidore saw that it was Corydon.

'Where is Pastorella?' eagerly asked Calidore.

Corydon burst into tears.

'Ah, well-a-day,' he said, 'I saw fair Pastorella die!'

He then told Calidore all about the robbers' raid, and all that had happened in that dreadful cave. Only one thing he did not know. He did not know that Pastorella was alive. He had seen her fall down, and he thought that she was dead.

So Calidore's heart was nearly broken, and he vowed a vow that he would not rest until he had punished the wicked men who had killed Pastorella.

He made Corydon come with him to show him the way to the robbers' island. At first Corydon was too frightened to go, but at last Calidore persuaded him. Together they set off, dressed like shepherds. But although Calidore carried only a shepherd's crook, under his smock he wore his steel armour.

When at last they had reached the island, they found some sheep grazing, and knew them for some of those that had belonged to Meliboeus. When Corydon saw the sheep he had taken care of in the days when he was most happy, he began to cry.

But Calidore comforted him, and they went on to where some robber shepherds lay asleep in the shade. Corydon wanted to kill them as they slept, but Calidore had other plans, and would not let him.

He awoke them, and they talked together. The robbers told him that they did not care to look after sheep, but liked better to fight and rob and kill. When Calidore and Corydon said that they would help them to keep the sheep, the robbers were glad. All day they stayed with the flocks, and at night the robbers took them home to their dark caves. There Calidore and Corydon heard news that made them glad, but made Calidore the more glad, for he loved Pastorella more than Corydon had ever done.

They learned that Pastorella was alive.

And so, day after day, they went on with their work, and waited and watched for a chance to set Pastorella free.

One night when the robbers had been away all day stealing and killing, and were all very tired, Calidore knew that the time had come to try to save Pastorella.

Corydon was too frightened to go with him. So all alone, at dead of night, Calidore went to the cave where the new robber captain, Pastorella's gaoler, slept. Calidore had managed to get a little sword belonging to a robber, but he had nothing else to fight with.

When he came to the cave, he found the door fastened. He put his strong shoulder against it, and burst the door in. The crash awoke Pastorella's gaoler, and he ran to see what it was. With one blow of his sword Calidore killed him. Then he called, till his voice rang through the gloomy cave, *'Pastorella!'*

Pastorella heard the noise, and lay trembling lest some new dreadful thing had come upon her. But when, again and again, Calidore called her name, her heart jumped for joy, and she ran out of the darkness right into her true knight's arms. And Calidore threw his arms about her, and kissed her a thousand times.

The robbers had waked up, hearing the crash of the door, and the yell of the robber as he died, and Calidore's cry of 'Pastorella.' Like a swarm of angry wasps they flocked to the door of the cave, but in the doorway stood Calidore with his sword, and slew every man who dared to try to kill him. He slew and slew until the doorway was blocked with dead bodies. Then those robbers that still lived were afraid to touch him, and went away to rest until morning.

Calidore also rested, and when daylight came he found amongst the dead robbers a better sword than the one he already had, and with that in his hand he walked out of the cave.

The robbers were lying in wait for him, and rushed at him from every side when he appeared.

But Calidore was like a lion in a herd of deer. With his sharp sword he thrust and smote, until the robbers who did not lie dead around him fled in terror, and hid themselves in their caves.

Then Calidore went back to where he had left Pastorella, and cheered and comforted her. Together they went through the robbers' caves, and took the richest of their treasures of gold and precious jewels. All the sheep they gave to Corydon, who gladly drove them away.

Then Calidore took Pastorella to the castle of one of his friends, a noble knight, whose gentle wife was called Claribel.

Calidore had to go to hunt the monster that he was pursuing when he first met the shepherds, so he left Pastorella with the knight and his lady. Pastorella was so gentle and beautiful that they loved her for her own sweet sake, as well as for Calidore's, and cared for her as if she was their own daughter.

An old woman who had always been Claribel's maid was given as maid to Pastorella.

One morning as this woman helped her to dress, she noticed on Pastorella's white breast a curious little mark. It was as if some one had painted on the fair skin a tiny purple rose with open petals. The old woman ran to her mistress, Claribel.

'Your baby lives!' she cried; 'the little baby I left crying under the green bushes is the beautiful Pastorella who is to marry Sir Calidore!'

Claribel ran to Pastorella's room, and looked at the little rose, and asked many questions. And when Pastorella had answered her, she was quite satisfied that she was indeed the baby-girl for whom her heart had been so hungry through all those years.

'My daughter, my daughter, that I mourned as dead!' she sobbed, as she held Pastorella in her arms and kissed her again and again.

When the knight knew that he was Pastorella's father, he was as glad as Claribel. So they lived happily together until

Calidore had slain the monster and come back to marry Pastorella.

Then instead of Pastorella, the shepherd's daughter, with her little dainty gown and her wreath of wildflowers, he found a Pastorella in jewels, and silks, and satins, who was the daughter of a great knight and his lady, and grand-daughter of the Lord of Many Islands.

Yet the Pastorella who married brave Sir Calidore was evermore Pastorella, the simplest and sweetest bride that any knight ever brought to the court of the Faerie Queen.

VI

CAMBELL AND TRIAMOND

Once upon a time a fairy had a lovely daughter called Cambina, and three sons who were born on the same day.

The eldest son she named Priamond, the second Diamond, and the third Triamond.

Priamond was very stout and big, but he could not strike hard. Diamond struck very hard, but he was little and thin. But Triamond was tall and stout and strong as well.

Priamond used to fight on foot. Triamond fought on horseback. But Diamond could fight equally well on a horse or off it.

Triamond fought with a spear and shield. Diamond fought with a battle-axe. But Priamond could fight just as well with an axe as he could with a spear and shield.

Their fairy mother was so fond and so proud of her gallant sons, that she could not bear to think of one of them dying.

So she went to see three witches called the Three Fates, who lived in a dark place underground, and worked at their spinning-wheels day and night. She asked the Fates to let her sons have long, long lives. That they would not promise, but they promised that if Priamond died first, all his strength should go into the other two. And if Diamond should then die, all his strength and Priamond's were to go into their brother Triamond.

Priamond, Diamond, and Triamond loved each other very dearly. When they grew up and all fell in love with the same lady, it did not make them less good friends.

The name of this lady was Canacee. She was very beautiful, and was the cleverest lady in all that land. She knew all about birds and beasts and plants and flowers, and was as witty as she was wise.

Many knights wished to marry her, and these knights were so jealous of each other that they were constantly fighting about her.

Canacee had a brother named Cambell, a wise young knight, who was sorry to see how often the knights fought with each other about his sister.

One day, when they were all gathered together, Cambell told them that he had made a plan by which they could decide which of them was to marry Canacee.

She asked the Fates to let her sons have long, long lives

'Choose from amongst yourselves,' said he, 'the three knights that you all think the bravest and the best fighters, and I shall fight them, one by one. The knight who beats me shall have my sister Canacee for his wife.'

Now all the knights knew that Canacee had given her brother a magic ring, and that, as long as he wore it, no matter how deep a wound he got, the wound would not bleed, and he would not die.

'It is very well for Cambell,' they said. 'We cannot kill him, but he can kill us.'

So they would not fight, even to win Canacee.

But the three brothers, Priamond, Diamond, and Triamond, were not afraid.

'We will fight with you, Cambell,' they said, 'for all of us love Canacee.'

So a day was fixed for this great fight. On the morning of the day, no sooner was it light than the three brothers in their shining armour were ready on the field. Crowds of people came to watch the fight, and there were six judges to see that the knights fought fairly. Canacee, in a beautiful dress, sat on a high platform whence she could see all that went on. When Cambell strode into the field, he looked as if he were quite sure of defeating all three knights.

Then came Priamond, Diamond, and Triamond, marching together, in splendid armour, with their gay-coloured banners flying.

They bowed low before Canacee, the lady they loved, and the trumpets sounded and sweet music played.

Then a trumpet blew loudly, and Cambell and stout Priamond began to fight.

Furiously they struck at each other, and at last Priamond's spear went through Cambell's shoulder. But although the shoulder was pierced, and the pain from the wound was terrible, not a single drop of blood fell from it. So they fought and fought, until Cambell's spear was driven through brave Priamond's neck. Like a great oak-tree that the storm has struck, Priamond tottered, then fell with a mighty crash. There, on the ground, he lay bleeding and dead.

When he died, all his strength passed into his two brothers, as the Three Fates had promised to his fairy mother.

A second time the trumpet sounded, and slight little Diamond, his battle-axe in his hand, fiercely rushed at Cambell.

So furiously did they hew and hack at each other, that their armour was cut and gashed as if it had been rotten wood. No blood flowed from Cambell's wounds, but Diamond's blood gushed fast, and reddened the green turf.

Fierce little Diamond grew tired at last of hacking and hewing and yet never killing Cambell. So he put all his strength into one terrible stroke, and swung his axe round with all his might. Had the blow reached Cambell it must have chopped his head in two, but Cambell swerved aside. Diamond had used so much force, that when he missed his aim his foot slipped. Cambell took the chance, let drive at him with all his power, and with his axe cut Diamond's head clean off.

For a moment Diamond's headless body stood still. Then gallant little Diamond fell dead on the ground. As he fell, all his strength, and the strength of Priamond, went into Triamond, the youngest brother.

Then Triamond, stronger and more angry than he had ever been before, lightly sprang up from where he had sat to watch the fight.

His strokes fell like hail on Cambell's armour. He struck, he thrust, he hewed, he hacked, till the sparks flew from his sword like the shining drops that are dashed from a waterfall.

Sometimes Triamond seemed to be winning; sometimes Cambell. The blood gushed from Triamond's wounds, till he grew faint. But although Cambell was covered with wounds the magic ring stopped his blood from flowing, so that he grew no less strong. When he saw Triamond growing weak, he smote him in the throat with all his might, and Triamond fell down as if he were dead.

But Triamond did not die. From the fearful wound all the strength that had belonged to his brother Priamond ebbed away. Still he had his own strength and Diamond's strength left.

So he rose up again, and Cambell, who had thought him dead, was so amazed that Triamond gave him a hard stroke before he had time to defend himself. Then Cambell fought with more care, and seemed rather to try to save himself than to try to kill Triamond. Triamond, seeing this, thought that Cambell must be tired, and that he could easily beat him now. With that he whirled up his sword to give a fearful blow. But Cambell, quick as lightning, thrust his sword under Triamond's upraised arm, so that it passed right through his body and came out at the other side. Even then the blow that Triamond struck was such a terrible one, that it cut through Cambell's steel helmet and gashed open his head, and he fell senseless to the ground.

Triamond, too, fell down, and out of his wound all Diamond's strength ebbed away.

When those who looked on saw this, they thought that the fight was at an end, because the fighters all lay dead.

Canacee began to cry because her brother and the brave knight who loved her were slain. But in a moment both knights rose to their feet again.

Those who watched could not believe their eyes when they saw them begin to fight as fiercely as before.

While every one stared in wonder and in fear, because they knew that soon the knights must surely kill each other, a loud noise suddenly drowned the clash of weapons.

It was a sound as of women and boys shouting and screaming in a panic.

Cambell and Triamond stopped their fight for an instant to listen and to look at the place from whence the noise came.

They saw a golden chariot, decked with wonderful ornaments, whirling towards them with the force of a storm. Two fierce lions drew the chariot, and in it sat a lady, whose face shone with beauty and goodness.

It was Triamond's sister, Cambina, who knew more about magic than almost any one else in all Fairyland.

When the crowds who watched saw her and her growling lions, they huddled together like frightened sheep. Some laughed, most of them screamed, and all of them ran till the dust flew up in clouds.

In one hand Cambina carried a magic wand with two serpents twisted round it. In the other she held a golden cup filled with a magic drink, that made those who drank of it forget all anger and bitterness, and filled their hearts with happiness and friendship and peace.

When Cambina came to the wooden barrier that shut off the watchers from the field where the knights had fought, she softly struck the rail with her wand.

It flew open, and the lions dashed in with Cambina's glittering chariot.

She got out of her chariot and ran up to the two knights, and begged them to fight no more. But they would not listen, and began to fight again.

Then she knelt on the bloodstained ground, and besought them with tears to lay down their swords. When they still went fiercely on, she smote them lightly with her magic wand.

Their swords fell to the ground, and while they stared at each other in wonder, Cambina handed them her golden cup. They were so hot and thirsty that they gladly drank. And, as they drank, all anger went out of their hearts, and love for each other took its place. They kissed, and shook hands, and vowed that they would be friends for evermore.

When the people saw this, they shouted and cheered for gladness till all the air rang.

And Canacee ran down from her platform and kissed Cambina, who had stopped the fearful fight and made Canacee's brother and her lover friends.

Then the trumpets sounded, and Cambina took Canacee into her chariot beside her, and the lions galloped off to Canacee's palace. And all the people thought how beautiful were these two lovely ladies, whose faces were fresh as morning roses and radiant with happiness.

Cambell and Canacee gave a great feast that lasted for days and days.

And Triamond married Canacee, and Cambell married
Cambina, and they all lived happily and peacefully ever
afterwards.

VII

MARINELL, THE SEA-NYMPH'S SON

Sometimes when the sun is rising on the sea and making the waves all pink and gold, the sailors whose boats are sailing out of the grey night fancy that they see fair ladies floating on the white crests of the waves, or drying their long yellow hair in the warm sunshine.

Sometimes poets who wander on the beach at night, or sit on the high cliffs where the sea-pinks grow, see those beautiful ladies playing in the silver moonlight.

And musicians hear them singing, singing, singing, till their songs silence the sea-birds harsh cry, and their voices blend with the swish and the rush of the sea and the moan of the waves on the shore.

The sailors tell stories of them, and the musicians put their songs into their hearts. But the poets write poems about them, and say:—

'There are no ladies so fair to see as the nymphs whose father is a king.
Nereus is their father, and they are the Nereids.
Their home is under the sea; as blue as the sea are their eyes.
Their long, long hair is yellow like sand.
Their silver voices are like lutes, and they steal men's hearts away.'

Long, long ago, one of these nymphs became the wife of a brave knight, who found her sleeping amongst the rocks and loved her for her beauty. Cymoënt was her name, and the other nymphs called her Cymoënt the Black Browed, because dark lashes and eyebrows shaded her sea-blue eyes.

The knight and the nymph had a son as strong and as brave as his father, and as beautiful as his mother, and Cymoënt called him Marinell.

'My son must be richer than any of the knights who live on the land,' said Cymoënt to the king her father. 'Give him riches.'

So the sea-king told the waves to cast on the shore riches that they had stolen from all the ships that had ever been wrecked. And the waves strewed the strand with gold and amber and ivory and pearls, and every sort of jewel and precious stone.

The shore sparkled and shone with Marinell's riches, and no one dared touch them, for Marinell had beaten a hundred knights in battle, and fought every man who dared venture to ride along these sands.

Cymoënt feared that as Marinell had won so many fights, he might grow reckless and get killed. Now Neptune, who was king of all the seas, had a shepherd who could tell what was going to happen in the future.

'Tell me,' Cymoënt said to him, 'how long my Marinell will live, and from what dangers he must take most care to keep away.'

'Do not let him go near any women,' said the Shepherd of the Seas. 'I can see that a woman will either hurt him very much, or kill him altogether.'

So Cymoënt warned her son never to go near any woman. And many ladies were sad because handsome Marinell would not speak to them, and the lovely lady Florimell was the saddest of all.

One day as Marinell proudly rode along the glittering sand, he saw a knight in armour that shone as brightly as the gold that the little waves had kissed.

'I am Lord of the Golden Strand!' said Marinell angrily, 'how dare the knight ride on the shore that is all my own!'

He rode furiously up, and told the knight to fly.

But the knight was Britomart, the fair lady with a man's armour and a man's heart. She scorned his proud words, and smote him with her magic spear.

And Britomart rode away, leaving Marinell lying as if he were dead.

His red blood stained his armour, and reddened the little waves that crept up to see what was wrong. The water washed over his feet.

'He is asleep,' said the little waves. 'We will wake him.'

But Marinell lay cold and still, and the blood dripped and dripped on to the golden sand.

Then the waves grew frightened, and the sea-birds screamed, '*Marinell is dead, is dead ... dead ... dead....*'

So the news came to his mother Cymoënt. Cymoënt and her sisters were playing by a pond near the sea, round which grew nodding yellow daffodils. They were picking the daffodils and making them into garlands for their fair heads, when they heard the message of the birds, '*Marinell is dead, dead, dead.*'

Cymoënt tore the daffodils from her hair, and fell on the ground in a faint. All her sister nymphs wailed and wept and threw their gay flowers away, and Cymoënt lay with white face, and her head on the poor, torn daffodils.

But the knight was Britomart, the fair lady with a man's armour and a man's heart

At last she came out of her faint, and asked for her chariot, and all her sisters sent for their chariots too.

A team of dolphins drew the chariot of Cymoënt, and they were trained so well that they cut through the water as swiftly as swallows, and did not even leave a track of white foam behind. Other fishes drew the chariots of the other nymphs, and Neptune, King of all the Seas, was so sorry for the sorrow of Cymoënt and the other Nereids, that he told his waves to be gentle, and let them pass peacefully to where Marinell lay on the golden strand.

When they got near where he lay, they got out of their chariots, for they feared that the dolphins and other fishes might get bruised and hurt by the rocks and pebbles on the shore. And with their strong white arms they swiftly swam to where Marinell lay, still and silent in his blood.

When Cymoënt saw her son's white face, she fainted again, and when she had recovered from her faint, she cried and moaned so bitterly, that even the hard rocks nearly wept for sorrow.

She and her sisters carefully looked at Marinell's wound, and one of them, who knew much about healing, felt his pulse, and found that a little life was still left in him. With their soft, silver-fringed mantles they wiped the blood from the wound, and poured in soothing balm and nectar, and bound it up. Then they strewed Cymoënt's chariot with flowers, and lifted Marinell gently up, and laid him in it. And the dolphins, knowing to go quietly and swiftly, swam off with Cymoënt and Marinell to Cymoënt's bower under the sea.

Deep in the bottom of the sea was the bower. It was built of hollow waves, heaped high, like stormy clouds. In it they laid Marinell, and hastily sent for the doctor of all the folk under the sea, to come and try to cure the dreadful wound.

So clever and so wise was this doctor, that soon the nymphs could laugh and sport again because Marinell was well.

But Cymoënt was afraid that some other harm might come to him if he went on to the land. So she made him stay beside her, under the sea, until Marinell grew tired of doing nothing. He longed to gallop away on his horse, his sword clanking by his side, and see the green woods and grey towers of the land, instead of idling away the hours in a bower under the sea, where there was nothing for him to do, but to watch the fishes of silver and blue and red, as they chased each other through the forests of seaweed.

One day two great rivers were married, and all the sea-folk went to the wedding. A feast was given in the house of the Shepherd of the Seas, and while Cymoënt and the other nymphs were there, Marinell wandered about outside. For because Marinell's father had been a knight and not one of the sea-folk, Marinell might not eat the food they ate.

While the feast went gaily on, Marinell heard piteous cries coming from under a black cliff. And when he listened, he knew that the voice was the voice of Florimell.

The wicked old Shepherd of the Seas had found her tossing on the waves in a little boat, and had taken her home to his deep-down caves to make her his wife. But Florimell did not love the old man. She loved only Marinell. So nothing that the shepherd could do would make Florimell say that she would marry him. At last, in a rage, he shut her up in a gloomy place under a dark rock, where no sunshine ever came.

'She will soon grow tired of the dark and the loneliness,' he thought, 'and then she will give in, and become my wife.'

But Florimell would not give in. She was crying and sobbing when Marinell came to the rock, and he heard her say, 'Marinell, Marinell, all this I suffer for love of thee.'

Marinell stood still and listened. Then he heard her say:—

'In spite of all this sorrow, yet will I never of my love repent,
But joy that for his sake I suffered prisonment.'

Then she gave yet more pitiful sobs, for she was very sad and cold and hungry. Yet always she would say again, between her sobs, 'I will never love any man but Marinell.'

Now Marinell had never in all his life truly loved any one. But when he heard Florimell's piteous voice, and knew how she loved him, and how much she had suffered for his sake, his heart, that had been so hard, grew soft.

'Poor little maid,' he said to himself, 'poor, beautiful little Florimell.'

No sooner had he begun to love Florimell, than he began to think of a plan by which to save her from the bad old shepherd.

At first, he thought he would ask the shepherd to let her go. But he knew that that would be no good. Then he thought that he would fight with the shepherd, and win her in that way. But that plan he also gave up. 'I will break into her prison, and steal her away,' he thought next. But he had no boat, and the sea flowed all round the rock, so that it was not possible.

While he still thought and planned, the marriage-feast came to an end, and Marinell had to go home with his mother. He looked so miserable that no one would have taken him for a wedding-guest.

Each day that passed after the wedding found him looking more and more sad. He could not eat nor sleep for thinking of Florimell, shut up in a dreary dungeon from which he could not free her. For want of sleep and food, and because he was so unhappy, Marinell grew ill. He was so weak that he could not rise, and his mother, Cymoënt, was greatly distressed.

'The wound he got from Britomart cannot be rightly healed,' she said. So she sent for the wise doctor of the seas.

'The old wound is quite whole,' said the doctor. 'This is a new pain which I cannot understand.'

Then Cymoënt sent for a doctor who was so wise and so great that he was chief of all the doctors on the land. When he had examined Marinell he said, 'The name of this illness is Love.'

Then Cymoënt begged Marinell to tell her which of the sea-nymphs it was that he loved.

'Whoever she is that you love,' she said, 'I shall help you to gain her for your wife.'

So Marinell told his mother that it was no nymph of the sea that had given his heart a deeper wound than ever Britomart's spear had dealt.

'I love Florimell,' he said, 'and she lies, a dreary prisoner, in the darkest cave of the Herd of the Seas.'

At first Cymoënt was sorry, for she did not wish her son to wed a maiden from the land. But when she knew how much Marinell loved Florimell, she went to Neptune, the King of all the Seas, as he sat on his throne, his three-pronged mace in his hand, and his long hair dripping with brine.

To him she told all the tale of Marinell and Florimell and the wicked old shepherd.

And Neptune wrote a royal warrant, and sealed it with the seal of the Sea Gods, commanding his shepherd to give up Florimell at once to Cymoënt the sea-nymph.

Thankfully Cymoënt took the warrant, and swiftly swam to the shepherd's sea-caves.

The shepherd was very angry, but all the sea-folk had to obey Neptune, so he sulkily opened the prison door and let Florimell go free.

When the black-browed Cymoënt took hold of the little white hand of the maiden her son loved, and looked on her lovely face, she was no longer sorry that Marinell did not wish to marry a sea-nymph. For no maiden in the sea was as beautiful or as sweet as Florimell.

She led Florimell to her bower, where Marinell lay so pale and weak and sad. And when Marinell saw Florimell standing blushing beside him, her hand in his mother's, all his sadness went away and his strength came back, and the pain in his heart was cured.

And if you listen some night when the stars are out, and the moon has made a silver path on the sea, you will hear the little waves that swish on the shore softly murmuring a little song. And perhaps, if your ears are very quick, and the big waves' thunder does not drown the sound of their melody, you may hear them whispering the names of two happy lovers, Florimell and Marinell.

VIII

FLORIMELL AND THE WITCH

In Fairyland, where all the knights are brave, and all the ladies beautiful, the lady who was once the most beautiful of all was called Florimell.

Many knights loved Florimell and wished to marry her. But Florimell loved only one, and he was Marinell, the son of a sea-nymph and a fairy knight And Marinell loved no one, not even Florimell.

Marinell was a bold knight, who had no sooner fought one fight than he was ready for another.

One day there was brought to the court news of his latest fight. Britomart, the maiden who feared no one, and who wore man's armour and carried a magic spear, had fought with Marinell, and Marinell was dead. So said they who brought the news.

'What will Florimell do?' whispered the court ladies, one to the other.

And all the knights were sad at heart for beautiful Florimell.

When Florimell was told what had befallen Marinell, she rose up from where she sat.

'I go to find him,' she said. 'Living or dead, I will find Marinell.'

Florimell had long, long golden hair. Florimell's eyes were blue as the sky, and her cheeks were pink, like the sweetest rose in the garden. A circlet of gold and jewels crowned her head. She mounted her snow-white palfrey with its trappings of gold, and rode away through the green woods to look for Marinell.

Four days she rode, but she did not find him. On the fourth day, as she passed through a lonely forest, a wicked robber saw her. He rode after her with his heavy boar-spear, and drove his spurs into the sides of his tired horse till the blood ran down.

When Florimell saw him, she made her palfrey gallop. Off it flew, like the wind, with the thud of the other horse's hoofs and the crash of branches to urge it on.

Florimell's golden hair flew behind her, till it looked like the shining track of a shooting star. Her face was white, and her frightened eyes shone like crystal.

Some knights who saw her flash through the trees on her white palfrey, like a streak of light, thought that she must be a spirit.

Florimell's golden hair flew behind her

But when they saw the ugly robber on his panting horse, they knew that he was real enough. They rode hard after him, and frightened him so much that he hid himself in the thickest part of the forest.

Florimell passed the knights without seeing them. And even after the robber had ceased to follow her, she fancied that she heard his rough voice and the thud of his horse's hoofs, and made her white palfrey go faster and yet more fast.

At last, as the palfrey tossed its head in its stride, it jerked the reins from out her tired little hands, and went on where it pleased.

All through the night they fled. The wild deer ran, startled, before them, and all the other beasts of the woods wondered at the sight of a white palfrey that galloped where it would under the grey boughs of the forest, carrying a lady whose hair gleamed like gold in the light of the stars. When rosy dawn had come, the horse stopped at last, too tired to do anything but stand and pant with foam-flecked mouth and heaving sides.

Then Florimell got off his back and coaxed him slowly on.

When they had wandered thus for hours, they came to a hill that shaded a thickly wooded valley. Over the tops of the tall trees in the valley Florimell saw a little blue curl of smoke. Glad at heart to think of finding a shelter and resting-place for her horse and herself, she led her palfrey towards it.

In a gloomy glen she found a little cottage built of sticks and reeds and turf. A wicked, ugly old witch and her wicked, ugly son lived in this hut. When Florimell came to the door, the old woman was sitting on the dusty floor, busy with some of her evil magic. When she looked up and saw beautiful Florimell, with her golden hair, and her face like a drooping white lily, she got a great fright. For she thought that Florimell was a good spirit come to punish her for all the bad things she had done.

But Florimell, with tears trickling down and making her face look like a lily in the dew, begged her, in gentle, pleading words, to give her shelter.

And so gentle and beautiful and sorrowful was Florimell, that, for the first time in the whole of her wicked life, the old witch felt some pity in her cruel heart. She told Florimell not to cry, and bade her sit down and rest. So Florimell sat down on the dusty floor and rested, as a little bird rests after a storm. She tried to tidy her robes that were rent by the branches and briars through which she had passed, and she smoothed her hair, and arranged her sparkling jewels.

The old hag sat and stared at her, and could not say a word, so much did she marvel at Florimell's wondrous beauty.

When it was midday, the witch's son came in. At the sight of Florimell he was as frightened as his mother had been, and stared in wonder and in fear. But Florimell spoke to them both so gently and so kindly that soon they no longer feared her.

She stayed with them in the wretched little hut for some time. And in that time the witch's son came to love her, and to long to have her for his wife. He tried to do everything that he thought would please her. He would bring her from the woods the rosiest of the wild apples, and the prettiest of the wildflowers he made into garlands for her hair. He caught young birds and taught them to whistle the tunes she liked, and young squirrels he caught and tamed and gave to her.

But Florimell feared both him and his wicked old mother. When her palfrey had rested, and grazed on the grass in the glen until it was quite strong once more, at daybreak one morning she put its golden trappings on again and rode away. She shivered at each shadow, and trembled at each sound, because she was so afraid that the witch or her son would follow her.

But these two wicked people slept until it was broad daylight and Florimell was far away. When they awoke and found her gone, they were furiously angry, and the witch's son was so frantic that he scratched his own face and bit himself, and tore at his rough long hair.

'I shall bring her back, or else kill her!' said the witch.

Then she went to a dark cave, and called out of it a horrible beast like a hyena. Its back was speckled with a thousand colours, and it could run faster than any other beast.

'Fetch Florimell back to me!' said the witch, 'or else tear her in pieces!'

Off the beast rushed, and before long it saw Florimell on her white horse riding through the trees.

There was no need to make the palfrey gallop when it saw the hideous beast with long, soft strides coming swiftly after it. The white palfrey went as fast as a race-horse, but the beast went as fast as the wind. As they came out of the forest, the beast's hot breath was close behind Florimell. And by that time her horse was so tired that its pace slackened. They had come to where there were no more trees, and in front of them lay yellow sand, and a long, long stretch of blue-green sea. When Florimell saw the sea, she leaped from her tired horse and ran and ran.

'I had rather be drowned,' she thought, 'than be killed by that loathsome monster.'

Now, an old fisherman had been drying his nets on the sand, and while they dried he slept in the bottom of his little boat, that lay heaving gently up and down in the shallows.

When Florimell saw this boat, she ran towards it and jumped in, and, with an oar, pushed it off into deeper water. The beast got to the water's edge just too late, for it was afraid of the sea and dared not follow her. In a rage it fell upon the white palfrey and tore it in pieces, and was eating it when a good knight who knew Florimell passed that way. He knew that the white horse was Florimell's, so he attacked the beast, and cut it and struck it so furiously with his sword that all its strength was beaten out of it and he could easily have killed it. But the knight thought that he would rather catch the strange beast and lead it home with him.

Lying on the sand near the dead white palfrey, he saw a golden girdle that sparkled with jewels, and that he had seen worn by Florimell. With this girdle he bound the beast, and led it after him like a dog. As he led it, he met a wicked giantess, and while he fought with her the beast escaped and ran away back to the witch's hut.

When the witch saw Florimell's jewelled girdle she was glad, for she thought that the beast must have killed Florimell. She ran with it to her son, but the sight of it, without Florimell, made him so angry that he tried to kill both the beast and his mother. The witch was so frightened that she set all her magic to work, to try to comfort her son. With snow and mercury and wax she made an image as like Florimell as she could. Its cheeks were rosy, like Florimell's, and she took two little burning lamps and put them in silver sockets, so that they looked just like Florimell's bright eyes. Her hair she made of the very finest golden wire. She dressed the image in some clothes that Florimell, in her flight, had left behind her, and round its waist she fastened Florimell's jewelled girdle. Then she put a wicked fairy inside the image, and told him to do his very best to act and to talk and to walk like Florimell. This image she then led to her son, and he thought it was the real Florimell come back, and was delighted. The false Florimell was not afraid of him as the real Florimell had been, and would walk in the woods with him, and listen, quite pleased, to all that he had to say.

But as they were in the forest one day, a bad knight saw them, and thought the false Florimell so beautiful that he seized her and rode away with her, and left the witch's son more sad and angry than ever.

When the real Florimell had escaped from the beast, the little boat that she pushed off from the shore went gaily sailing onward and onward with the tide. They were far out at sea when the old fisherman awoke. He got a great fright when he found himself far from the shore, and with a lovely lady beside him. But he was a very bad old man, and when he saw Florimell's fine jewels and beautiful clothes he thought he would rob her. He knocked her down into the bottom of his boat amongst the fishes' scales, and might have killed her, had not Florimell screamed and screamed for help. There was no ship near, and the waves and the sea-birds could not help her.

But it chanced that the shepherd of all the flocks in the sea was driving his chariot that way. He was an old man with long white hair and beard. Sometimes on a stormy day one may see him far out at sea, as he drives his flocks that look from far away like snowy froth and foam.

When the shepherd saw the wicked fisherman struggling with Florimell, he beat the old robber so hard with his staff that there soon was very little life left in him. Then he lifted Florimell, all tearful and trembling, into his chariot. When she could only cry, he gently kissed her. But his lips were frosty cold, and icicles from his long white beard dropped on to her breast and made her shiver.

He took her to his home in a hollow rock at the bottom of the sea, and he asked her to be his wife.

'I cannot marry you,' said Florimell. 'I do not love you. My only love is Marinell.'

Then the cunning old shepherd by magic made himself look like a fairy knight, and thought that Florimell would love him.

'I do not love you. I love Marinell,' still was Florimell's answer.

He then tried to frighten Florimell and make her marry him, whether she would or not. He turned himself into dreadful shapes—giants, and all sorts of animals and monsters. He went inside the waves, and made terrifying storms rage. But nothing that he might do would make Florimell consent to marry him.

At last he imprisoned her in a dark cavern.

'She will soon tire of that, and then she will marry me,' said he to himself.

But Florimell said the more, 'I love only Marinell. I am glad to suffer, because I suffer for Marinell's dear sake.'

She might have died there, and been buried under the sea-flowers of scarlet and green, and had the gay little fishes dart over her grave, and none might ever have known.

But, by happy chance, Marinell came that way. He heard her voice coming out of her prison far beneath the sea, like the echo of a sad song, and suddenly he knew that he loved her.

The sea-nymph, his mother, told Neptune, King of the Seas, that his shepherd had imprisoned a beautiful maiden in his darkest cave, and begged him to set Florimell free, that she might become Marinell's wife.

So Florimell was set free at last, and all her troubles were ended.

Marinell took her away from the kingdom under the sea back to Fairyland, and they were married in a castle by the golden strand. Every beautiful lady and every brave knight in Fairyland was there. They had tournaments every day, and each knight fought for the lady he thought the most beautiful and loved the best.

Marinell was victor in every fight but one, and in this he was beaten by another brave knight. This knight had on his shield a device of a blazing sun on a golden field.

When he had fought and won the prize, this shield was stolen from him by the wicked knight who had run away with the false Florimell. No one could see the faces of the knights, for their helmets covered them. So when the wicked knight came forward, carrying the blazing shield, and pretended that he had won the prize, Florimell, who was queen of the revels, handed him the victor's garland, and praised him for having fought so well.

'I did not fight for you!' roughly answered the knight. 'I would not fight for you! I fight for one more beautiful.'

Florimell blushed for shame, but before any one could answer him, the knight drew forward the false Florimell and threw back her veil.

And even Marinell could not tell that she was not his own beautiful bride that he loved so dearly, so exactly like the real Florimell had the witch made the image.

Just then the knight whose shield had been stolen pushed through the crowd.

'You false coward with your borrowed plumes!' he cried. 'Where is the sword you pretend that you fought with? Where are your wounds?'

With that he showed his own bloody sword, and his own bleeding wounds, and every one knew that the wicked knight had lied when he said that it was he who had won the fight.

'This is not the real Florimell!' said the brave knight of the blazing shield, pointing at the image. 'It is a wicked fairy, who is a fit mate for this base coward. Bring forward Florimell the bride, and let us see them side by side!'

So Florimell, blushing till her face looked like a nosegay of roses and lilies, was led forward, and stood beside the image of herself. But no sooner did she come near the image, than the image melted away, and vanished altogether. Nothing of it was left but the girdle of gold and jewels that Florimell had lost on the day she escaped from the witch's hut. And this the brave knight picked up, and clasped round Florimell's waist. The wicked knight had his armour taken from him, and was beaten until he ran howling away.

And Florimell, the fairest lady in all Fairyland, lived happily ever after with her gallant husband, Marinell, the Lord of the Golden Strand.

Made in the USA
Columbia, SC
01 June 2021